A SECOND CHANCE ON SNOW RIDGE

SNOW RIDGE SHIFTERS #1

L.E. WILSON

EVERBLOOD PUBLISHING

<u>**The Sergones Coven (Dragon Shifters & Vampires)**</u>

Dance for the Dragon

Burn for the Dragon

ISBN: 978-1-945499-67-8

Print Edition

Publication Date: April 28, 2022

Copy Editor: Jinxie Gervasio @ jinxiesworld.com

Cover Design by Dar at WickedSmartDesigns.com

CHAPTER 1

Of all the possible ways Riko thought this little adventure would end, one thing he hadn't ever considered was that he'd end up ass-over-elbow in a snare trap, swinging back and forth from a tree branch like an old man's ball sack.

Not five minutes ago, he'd left his truck on the side of the road, wanting to walk a little and breathe the crisp air as he followed the centerline of the road that led into Fairplay, Colorado. A place he'd once thought of as home.

The sun was barely peeking over the horizon, but he'd already been driving for hours, trying to get a leg up on the snowstorm he could smell in the air. Up until today, it had been unusually warm in the mountains for this far into the winter, but otherwise, the place hadn't changed a bit in all the years he'd been gone.

And it still smelled like cow shit, just as he remembered it, even though there were no cows left. They'd all been wiped out, thanks to human greed and a raging virus that roared through factory farms one by one, taking down every animal in its path. Most people wouldn't associate the odor of manure to a place this close to a high-dollar ski resort—Breckenridge was just twenty-six miles north of the ranch—but Colorado was actually known for its cattle.

Or, at least, it had been.

Something crashed through the trees to his right and he froze. Reaching up over his shoulder, he pulled his weapon of choice from the homemade holder he'd made—mostly just some pieces of worn leather he'd pieced together—and hefted it in his right hand. The weapon was an Estwing E45A axe. He liked it because it had a long handle and a little more weight, it was forged all in one piece, and he could really get a lot of momentum behind his swing.

Muscles tense and ready, he waited for whatever it was to reveal itself. It sure was making a hell of a lot of noise. Maybe it was a bear. Or a moose. Too much for a shifter. Even an entire pack wouldn't come crashing through the trees like that.

Unless they *wanted* him to hear them.

Riko cursed himself for not taking the time to shift before he'd started out this morning from his camp. He'd known he was taking a chance entering this territory in his human form, but to be honest, he really didn't think anyone would be up and around this early. And if they were, and he happened to run across anyone, he'd assumed they might actually take the time to say good morning, maybe offer him a cup of coffee, and find out who the hell he was before they showed him why it had been a foolhardy idea to come back to this part of the country. Hell, if he was lucky, they might even give him a minute to explain why he hadn't been left with much of a choice.

Branches cracked and swayed just a few feet into the underbrush, and after a quick glance over his shoulder to make sure nothing had snuck up behind him, Riko backed up a few steps and did a few practice swings, loosening up his shoulder. Then he waited.

The low-hanging branches rustled, a few leaves shaking loose and falling to the ground. A second later, a large black nose poked through the mettle of branches right about at chest level. The thing in the bushes snuffed out a phlegm-filled huff of air, and with one good heave, pushed its way through, exposing a dirty, white face and thick, brown hide. It burst out onto the road right in front of Riko, hooves click-clacking on the pavement as it caught its balance and righted itself.

They both froze. Riko couldn't possibly be seeing what he thought he was seeing. There were no more cows left on any of the ranches. Not anywhere in the whole country. Maybe the whole world.

Except, apparently, this one.

His mouth began to water. As if the creature knew what he was about, it bellowed a deep warning moo, turned, and took off down the road, tail standing straight up and waving like a flag. Shaking off the shock factor, Riko took off after it, axe at the ready. There was no way in hell he was letting this meal get away. An animal that size would feed him for the next six months, maybe more, if he could find a good-sized freezer, or at least some salt to preserve the meat.

The bovine ran about thirty yards, then veered sharply to the right and entered an overgrown field.

Arms pumping, thighs burning, and his pack of supplies thumping hard against his back, Riko chased after it. The fucking thing was a lot faster than it looked. Who knew that an animal that spent most of its time wandering around chewing on regurgitated grass while staring dreamily into space could run like its life depended on it?

Which it did.

The toe of his boot caught in a tangle of long grass and Riko stumbled but didn't fall. Hacking at the offensive stuff with his axe, he ripped his foot out of the mess, watching as the cow got farther and farther away from him.

"Dammit!"

With a quick look around, he took off running again, this time heading toward the copse of trees on his right. He recognized this field from his days as a kid, and if he wasn't mistaken, he'd be able to cut off the cow on the other side and claim his meal, as long as it kept following the obvious path through the fields. His cousins used to fall for it every time.

Childish laughter echoed through Riko's head, long lost remnants of another time. Another life. He shook his skull hard, chasing away the memories. There was no going back to that life, and he'd damned well better remember that while he was here. As soon as his father was buried and a new alpha was chosen, he was getting the hell out of there. This was not his home anymore.

Refocusing, Riko ducked and weaved through the trees, avoiding low-hanging branches and leaping over rocks and other debris like a champion obstacle racer. Sweat beaded on his brow, and he shook it away before it could drip into his eyes and blind him. Just ahead, he saw the break in the trees he was looking for, and the field just beyond that.

And his fucking steak dinner.

The damn cow was still moving, though it *had* slowed down to a nervous trot. Every few seconds, it would swing its large head around, looking for him. But the thing was smart. It didn't assume the coast was clear and it could go back to grazing. It just didn't know where the threat was. But it knew was still there.

Riko slowed down just a bit and crept up to the edge of the tree line, his eye on his meal. He checked his grip on the axe, swapping hands and wiping his palms on his jean clad thighs. One slip, and the cow would be off again. His stomach protested the thought—loudly—and he wrapped his free arm around his waist, as though he could tamp down the hunger pangs with nothing but willpower.

Completely focused on the animal, who had finally slowed to a meandering walk, Riko crept forward, stepping heel to toe in order to make as little noise as possible. He kept his breaths shallow, forced his heartbeat to slow, and took his time. If he fucked this up, he'd be eating rabbit again tonight.

It occurred to him that it would be somewhat of a challenge to transport an entire cow the rest of his journey with only the pack on his back, but he'd figure something out.

A branch snapped under his foot, and Riko froze, his eyes on his prize. The cow froze, also. The ear closest to Riko pivoted like a radio antenna trying to catch a signal, and then a nervous shudder started near its head and worked its way all the way down to its tail, which gave a sharp swish.

Riko waited a few seconds, his heart pounding so loud he wondered how those big ears didn't hear it. Carefully, he slid one foot forward a few inches and took a step. Then two. Three. He lifted the axe, each finger lifting and re-gripping the handle again.

Four...

And suddenly, the world went topsy-turvy. A hoarse shout escaped his lungs as the ground disappeared and cold air rushed past his face as Riko was flung straight up in the air a good twenty feet. He paused, suspended in space for a second like a cartoon animation, before gravity took hold and down he went, dropping like a rock. Three seconds later, he came to an abrupt halt, coarse rope criss-crossing his body and biting into his arms, legs, and ass as he swung lazily back and forth in the air. Luckily, his supply pack protected his back.

It wasn't a freak tornado that had grabbed him up. It was a fucking booby trap. Homemade, from the looks of the net, but effective, nevertheless, as Riko had found out.

"Son of a bitch!" he shouted at the top of his lungs to any and all who were listening. And then remembering where he was, he dropped his voice and cursed some more, choosing a colorful array of words that would've sent his mother—bless her soul—running for the soap.

Riko struggled to twist his body around, finally managing to get his face between two of the ropes and watched—his stomach clenched—as the cow ran off willy-nilly through the fields.

"Fuck!" He twisted back around and pounded his fists against his thighs. "Fuck, fuck, FUCK!" Suddenly, it occurred to him—he didn't have his axe. Leaning forward, he spread his thighs and searched the ground beneath him.

There it was. A glint of steel lying amongst the leaves and twigs that had hid the trap he dangled in.

But Riko hadn't survived this long by depending only on his axe, although it *was* his favorite. As shifting wasn't an option in this position—these were brand new jeans he was wearing—he pulled his right pant leg up, exposed the top of his old combat boot, and dug around for the small blade he'd shoved down inside before he'd set out that morning. Not wasting any time thinking about how much gravity was going to hurt, he set to work on the ropes.

"Wrecking my teenage years wasn't enough for you, so now you're back to fuck up my trap?"

A sweet scent assailed him. A familiar scent. One that brought back a world of memories he'd just as soon forget. As the net spun in a slow circle, Riko stopped cutting and twisted his torso around, craning his neck to see.

A girl stood below him. No, not a girl. She wasn't a girl at all anymore, but a woman who had grown into her own skin, with all of the curves and swagger that had been lacking all those years ago. Her dark hair was pulled back from her face, showing off high cheekbones, and soft, wispy hairs curled around her neck.

"Addison?" He tried and failed to keep the shock and relief out of his voice. "Addison Conley? What the hell are you doing out here alone in the middle of the woods?"

She tipped her head to the side and regarded him with narrowed, hazel eyes. "Well, I was hoping to catch something for dinner," she said dryly. "But then you stumbled into the trap it took me all day to make." She sighed dramatically.

"You set up this trap?"

"Why do you sound so surprised?"

"I'm just...surprised is all." Riko shoved his knife back down into his boot. "Let me down from here, will you?"

She bent down and picked up his axe, testing its weight in both hands before she shoved it into the canvas bag she had slung across her body. "No. I don't think so."

"No?" Riko spoke more to himself than to her. Maybe it was the incessant noise his stomach was making that had blocked his hearing. "What the hell do you mean, 'no'?" he shouted.

"I mean, you're a pig. And an ass. And I'm leaving you up there to contemplate the lives you've ruined." She started walking away, stopped, and turned back to him. "Think of it this way. At least if any hunters wander by, they won't shoot you on sight since you're already in the net and all." She smiled. "See? I've already done you more favors than you ever did for me. You're welcome." Then she turned on her heel and walked away.

Riko scoffed, not quite believing she was just going to leave him there. He'd come all this way. Risked his fucking life. There was no way she would leave him hanging like this.

No way.

She wouldn't do it.

The rope creaked in the cold as he spun in a slow circle, his head turning first one way and then the other as he watched her walk away.

With his favorite axe.

Well, hell. She was leaving him there. Pulling out his knife again, he went back to work on the rope. He would fix her damn net later. She wouldn't even need the fucking thing if she hadn't fucked up his cow hunting. "Nice fucking hello," he mumbled. "She could at least pretend she was glad to fucking see me." His gut ached, but it was only from a lack of food, not because the female he'd never gotten completely out of his head had, quite literally, just left him hanging.

He sawed at the ropes until there was a big enough hole for his body to fit through. With one eye on the curvy figure of Addison growing smaller and smaller in the distance, he shoved the knife back into his boot. Maneuvering onto his hands and knees—no easy task, mind you—he pulled the net beneath him forward, slowly making his way to the hole he'd created. Hanging on tight, he twisted and bent his body in half, coming out ass first until his feet broke free and he was swinging by his fingertips fifteen feet off the ground. With a soft curse, he let go and dropped. He hit hard and rolled, somehow managing not to twist an ankle or break a wrist. Either injury would heal quickly, but it would still hurt.

Running his hands through his hair to get it out of his eyes, he adjusted his pack and set out after her. He didn't bother wasting energy by running. He could still see her through the tall grass.

Besides, he knew where she was going.

As he followed her down the old worn path, he wondered why the hell a human woman as gorgeous as Addison was still in this town. Was she married? Was that it? Had she settled down with one of the ranchers? Maybe had a few kids? Did she get into bed every night with a guy who was more interested in the TV than the piece of perfection lying next to him?

A low growl rumbled through Riko's chest at the thought of her in bed with another male. He didn't like it.

However, he had no say in who that woman slept with every night or what she did in any other part of her life, and he never would. Addison wasn't a shifter. And that meant she was off limits. Back in high school he didn't give two fucks about that. His only concern was getting his dick wet. But they weren't teenagers anymore, and actions had consequences now.

Something he would do well to remember.

Riko sighed as she headed straight toward town, such as it was. He would bet good money not a damn thing had changed since he'd taken off at the ripe old age of seventeen, with nothing but the clothes on his back, an attitude, and a resolution that he would find a new pack and never come back to this place.

And yet, somehow, when he'd gotten the news that the alpha had passed on, he'd found himself traveling north. The place where he'd been born and raised until he'd found the quickest way to get the hell out of there.

Population before he'd left? Probably exactly the same as it was now. A town where everyone knew everyone, along with their parents and grandparents and distant cousins, and gossip traveled faster than the speed of light. Hell, a guy couldn't take a piss in the woods without the whole goddamn town knowing about it five seconds later. Humans and shifters alike.

Riko stayed within the trees and watched as Addison entered the outskirts of Fairplay's "historic" downtown. The stretch of buildings had always reminded Riko of a movie set from the Old West. A bunch of rough and ramble shacks with façade store fronts.

Just like the people who lived there.

He kept his ears open and his eyes on the seductive sway of Addison's hips as she strolled down the middle of the empty street.

Maybe later he'd go back out and look for that cow.

CHAPTER 2

Addison pressed the palms of her hands to her cheeks, trying to cool them. Her face felt like it was on fire, and it only got worse the more she thought about the man she'd just caught in her trap.

What the hell was Riko fucking Silvano doing back here? And looking way better in his late thirties than he ever had in high school? Even with his long body bundled up in a winter coat and bent in half inside that net she could see that.

She rubbed her eyes with the heels of her hands, as though she could scrub the image of his fine ass from them with sheer force of will, but it was no use. If anything, the memory was even more vivid with her eyes closed. His black hair was longer than she remembered, falling over his wide forehead, and he had a close-cut beard covering his hard jawline. But his dark eyes were just as piercing. And they still made her entirely too aware of herself as a woman...

Snapping them back open, she sidestepped the parked car she'd almost walked into and pulled her own coat tighter so she could zip it up against the wind, then adjusted the strap of her bag on her shoulder. The temperature was really starting to drop. Maybe they'd get that snow tonight after all.

And maybe she should go back and check on Riko. Her steps slowed as she contemplated how bad she would feel if he froze to death in that net and was surprised to realize that it would actually be quite a lot.

But then she remembered what an asshole he'd been back in the day—and probably still was—and, thankfully, the feeling passed. Besides, he was a grown ass man. He'd figure it out.

Turning up a side street, Addison started up the incline toward the old, white farmhouse she still lived in with her father. Pushing all thoughts of Riko the asshole from her mind, she plastered a smile on her face and climbed the two steps to the porch, careful not to step where the wood had rotted. She stomped the snow and dirt from her boots and pulled open the creaky screen door, then shouldered open the storm door, which was unlocked. "Dad? I'm home."

The house was eerily silent.

"Dad?"

Pushing the heavy door mostly shut with her foot, she kicked off her boots and hung her bag and coat on the hook on the wall. In the kitchen, she found a note on the butcher block counter and picked it up, scanning her father's handwriting telling her he'd gone to hang out with Butch, his best bud since they'd both lost their wives.

"So, you were just gonna leave me there in that net for the bears to eat, huh?"

Her heart pounding, Addison spun around to find Riko leaning casually against the archway. "Get out of my house."

One corner of his mouth lifted into that same knowing smirk she remembered from high school. The one that made her stomach flutter and her palms sweat. His eyes ran over her, slow and purposeful, taking in her bulky sweater and old jeans, all the way down to her mismatched socks. But she could've been wearing nothing at all by the way they flared with heat.

"I mean it, Riko. Get out," she repeated a little more forcefully. Nothing good would come from this man standing in her kitchen.

"I just wanted to say I'm sorry," he told her.

Addison frowned, both at the smirk that was still on his face and the lack of sincerity in his tone. "For what? Ruining my trap?"

His smile widened. "No, although I will fix it for you."

"Then what?"

He paused, looking down at the floor so she couldn't read his expression. When he looked back up, all signs of amusement had left his face, and his eyes were actually sort of earnest when he said, "For leaving the way I did."

Remnants of past emotions seeped into her chest. Shame, loneliness, anger, and underneath it all, a whole lot of pain. She had to clear her throat before she could say anything. "That was a long time ago. It doesn't matter now."

He stared at her for a long time, then he pushed himself away from the wall, never taking his eyes from her. "I guess you're right. But still, I was an ass. And I just wanted to put that out there."

"I barely remember," she lied. "I've lived a whole other life since then."

That damn smirk reappeared as he glanced around her kitchen. "I don't know about that. Looks like the exact same life to me."

He was right. She still lived in the same house in the same town. Still knew the same people. Hell, she even wore the same clothes. Well, not the same size, but the same type of clothes. But she couldn't leave her father here all by himself, as much as she wanted to. And it was too late now to get out. Too late to start over somewhere else. "It was a life without you in it, and I liked it that way."

A flash of something darkened his eyes—hurt, maybe?—before he gave her an uncomfortable laugh, shoving his hands into the front pockets of his jeans. "Yeah, well. I couldn't wait to get out of here."

"Why are you back?" Addison made an effort to loosen the tension in her shoulders without making it obvious that his presence caused any kind of reaction in her at all.

"My father died."

She immediately felt like an ass. "I'm so sorry." How had she not known that? News traveled between houses faster than high-speed internet in this place. But, then again, his family had always been kind of hermit-like, living off in the mountains as they did. "When is the funeral?"

"The day after tomorrow."

"And then you're leaving again?" Ugh. That was cold. Even for her. She knew this. Still, she refused to show him any weakness, and waited expectantly for him to answer.

"In a few days," he told her with a tight smile.

It was what she'd hoped for. Addison didn't need this particular blast from the past stampeding back into her life and messing with her. He'd been nothing but a flash in the pan in the story of her life. And that's where he needed to stay.

So, why was her chest aching like she was seventeen again?

Shaking it off, she wondered if she'd be expected to go. Dead people gave her the creeps. Besides, although she knew Riko from school, she'd never met his family. And he'd been gone for twenty years.

"You don't have to go. But I appreciate the condolences."

"That's not what I was thinking."

"Yeah, it was." He held up his hand when she opened her mouth to deny it. "It's okay, Addi. It's not like you knew my father."

The nickname caught her off guard. "Don't call me that."

"Why not?" he countered. "It's your name."

Riko was the only one who'd ever called her that. "No, it's not. It's the name of a girl you wanted me to be. And that girl died a long time ago." *The day you left without saying goodbye.* She hadn't even known he was gone until one of the girls told her three weeks later.

"Aww, see. I'm gonna have to disagree with you there. Because I still see that girl standing right in front of me. A little grumpier, maybe," he teased. "But you're still the same girl, Addi. The girl I could never take my eyes from."

"That's bullshit, and you know it." She had no patience for his games. And he was an idiot if he thought he could still win them. "You barely noticed me until..." She couldn't bring herself to say the rest. *Until the night after graduation, when you didn't have to worry anymore about what anyone would think about you hooking up with me because you were about to leave.*

"Sure I did. You were the most popular girl in school. The head cheerleader. The prom queen. Everyone noticed you. I noticed you, Addi." His voice dropped on that last, pulling her into him and making the few feet that separated them much more intimate. "But unlike everyone else, I think I was the only one who saw the girl underneath all of that."

Why was he telling her all of this?

He took a step toward her. "I still notice you."

"Does it matter?"

Riko became very still, and the light in his eyes dulled. "No. I guess it doesn't."

Because I'm still not good enough for you. Got it. "Anything else you need to get off your chest? I have things to do."

He gave a slow shake of his head. "Nah. I think I'm good."

She stared at him pointedly, holding herself rigidly still as she waited for him to get the point.

Her heart picked up again as Riko started to turn away, but then he paused. "I'll get that net fixed for you and leave it on the porch."

"Don't worry about it. I have more traps. But you might wanna watch where you walk from now on if you're going to be wandering aimlessly around the woods."

"I happened to be chasing a cow. The only one I've seen in the last three years." His face lit up. "You wouldn't happen to know anything about it?"

Addison completely forgot about her previous issues with him in the light of this new piece of information. "You were after Mistletoe? Why?"

"Why?" He looked at her as if she'd lost her mind. "To eat! You know how long it's been since I had a steak dinner? In case you haven't noticed, Addi, there's no meat left in the world."

She crossed her arms and rolled her eyes. "There's plenty of meat. There's just no cows."

"Except for Mistletoe."

"Except for Mistletoe. And you're not allowed to eat her."

"Why the hell not?"

"Because she's mine. And I said you can't eat her."

He stared at her for a long moment. "Okay. So...what? Are you saving her for a special occasion?"

What the hell was it with men and steak? "No. I'm saving her because she's part of my family and I'm not going to let anyone eat her."

"Then why do you let her roam around on her own just looking for someone to hang her in their barn?"

Addison shrugged. "She gets out of the pasture sometimes. But everyone around here knows her, and no one will hurt her."

He gave her a funny look. "You better hope she doesn't wander off too far, or she might not come home one day."

"Are you threatening my cow?"

The smirk was back on his face, and Addison's palm itched with the urge to slap it off. "Not at all, sweetheart. Just stating facts."

"You can leave now," she informed him.

"Already halfway out the door," he quipped. With one last once over of her stiff figure, he strode out of her house, pulling the storm door closed behind him.

Addison listened to the heavy tread of his boots as he crossed the porch, not moving until he was off the steps and a good halfway across the lawn. Once she was sure he was gone, she hurried over to the door, only to find he'd locked it behind him when he'd left.

Walking over to the window, she moved the curtain out of the way and watched him as he headed back toward town, the Rocky Mountains creating a picturesque view before him. It looked like the final scene of a movie, with the hero walking away to go back to his adventurous life, never to think of the poor woman he was leaving behind or the heartbreak he left in his wake.

Only this was no movie; this was real life. And Addison wasn't about to let him break her heart again.

CHAPTER 3

The snow started to come down in light flurries just as Riko left Addison's house, and he suddenly had a raging case of *déjà vu*, because it had been snowing just like this the last time he'd seen her, twenty years ago.

Riko kept his eyes open as he headed back out of town to where he'd left his truck. He walked as fast as he could, his strides long and his footsteps quiet, his pulse pounding so hard in his ears he couldn't hear anything else. The same reaction he'd always had whenever he got anywhere near that woman.

It'd been stupid to follow Addison home. And even more asinine to corner her in her kitchen. The woman did things to him. Always had. And it looked like she always would. His obsession with her was the reason he'd taken off after high school and fought his way into a new shifter pack.

Well, not the only reason, but a big ol' part of it.

He made it to Main Street in record time and forced himself to slow down. It'd been a stupid idea to come back here. This wasn't his home anymore. It wasn't his pack. Everyone had moved on with their lives and he wasn't a part of them anymore. Yet, he'd come running the second he'd heard they'd lost their alpha.

He wasn't just your old alpha, he was your old man, dumbass.

A father he'd barely spoken to since his mother died in an accident fourteen years ago. So, yeah, no. He wasn't the reason Riko came back. And it wasn't because he was the only son and dominant enough to be next in line for the throne.

Oh, no. He could lie to himself all he wanted. But the truth was the truth. And the real reason he came back here—he could admit to himself now—had just ordered him to leave her house and wanted nothing to do with him. Not that he could blame her.

He honestly didn't know what he'd been thinking. Hell, the only things he should be concerned about were his new pack in Oklahoma and the alpha that recently took over. Keegan McRae, in the short time Riko had known him, appeared to be a badass wolf. Tough but fair. And he cared about his wolves. A vast improvement from their previous alpha, and Riko should be there with everyone else, claiming his position within the pack.

His mind (and every single cell in his body), however, was focused on the one thing he shouldn't be thinking about at all—Addison Conley.

As a teenager, Addi had been smart, popular, pretty, and was always smiling. All the time. She'd made his heart stop every time he walked out of class and saw her coming down the hallway.

As a grown woman, she was suspicious, prickly, argumentative...and the most irresistible thing Riko had ever had the pleasure of being within three feet of.

Funny enough, all of her efforts to chase him off only made her more attractive to him. He wanted to tangle his fingers in her thick, chocolate-brown hair and drag her back to Oklahoma with him, all caveman-style, and take his time getting to know every luscious curve that bulky sweater she was wearing only hinted at. He wanted to spend time with her. Argue with her. Laugh with her. Talk to her. Get her opinion on stuff he wasn't sure about. Get to know her again.

And that was why he needed to get the hell out of here as fast as he could.

Yup, good plan.

Despite his determination to get his mind back on the reason he was supposed to be there—his father's funeral —it took him the entire walk back to his truck to succeed even moderately. But it only took him another minute to realize Addi still had his favorite axe in her bag.

Son of a bitch!

Riko stopped walking, his hands fisting at his sides. But then he took a deep breath and relaxed his grip. She could have the damn thing. He'd just buy another one. He would NOT use this as an excuse to see her again.

Nope.

Wasn't happening.

Once he'd crested the hill and was safely under the cover of trees again, he turned around to look back at the town he'd grown up in. The damn cow was a few streets over from the main street, calmly walking up the empty sidewalk in front of what used to be some of the nicest houses in town, stopping now and again to forage where the weeds had taken over the small yards.

Watching it graze, Riko scowled, then turned around and continued to his truck. He'd have to drive further into the mountains to find the werewolf pack. And he needed to get his head on straight before he did. He'd been gone a long time, and the Central Colorado Pack wasn't known for their warm welcomes.

When he finally reached his truck, Riko climbed in and smiled as the engine roared to life. The black, lifted Chevy Silverado was probably a bit of overkill, but he loved it, and it got him where he needed to go.

Like now.

Riko checked his mirrors, pulled back onto the road, and continued up CO-9 toward Hoosier Pass. Once there, he'd pull off at the hiking trails and go the rest of the way on foot. If things still ran the way they used to, he was bound to run into some wolves out on patrol. And they would know he was there as soon as they got anywhere within a quarter mile from him if the wind was blowing the right way to carry his scent.

Twenty-five minutes later, Riko was on foot and heading off the trail to go deeper into the mountains. It was a bit of a hike, and despite the fact he'd grown up there, the altitude was making it a little hard to breathe. He was about eleven thousand feet above sea level now, and it was only going to get worse. Luckily, as a shifter, he'd adapt quicker than most.

He'd hiked about a mile when he heard it—a warning growl.

Immediately, Riko stopped walking, turning in the direction he'd heard the sound. He saw nothing at first, but then he caught a movement out of the corner of his right eye and whipped his head in that direction, catching and holding the eyes of the large, gray wolf who was standing about fifty feet away near a large boulder. A little too far to recognize if he knew the male or not. Although he'd purposefully stayed in his human skin so as not to seem threatening, his natural dominance vibrated under his skin as he waited for the other wolf to lower its eyes.

He didn't.

Instead, it stalked closer, its upper lip lifted in a snarl as its yellow eyes drilled right into Riko's with no sign of fear. Behind it, three more wolves appeared from within the trees. Slightly smaller, but no less aggressive than the large wolf in the lead.

Well, shit.

A group of wolves acting this way could only mean one thing, there was no alpha leading this pack. Which meant there wasn't any one wolf whose dominance had been enough to groom him for the position.

This was a rogue pack of wolves.

Tilting his head side to side, Riko cracked his neck, shook the tension out of his arms and legs, and without thinking too hard about it, took off down the mountain back toward the path. He chose his footing carefully, avoiding any loose gravel that would send him toppling, and made it to the bottom without any issues. Riko paused, hidden within the trees, and listened for a split second to see if they were giving chase. When he heard nothing, he peeked out from behind the large tree trunk he was hiding behind.

Four wolves were running silently down the mountain.

"Fuck! Fuck! Fuck!" No longer trying to be stealthy, Riko ran full out around a few large rocks and headed down the mountain. He didn't look back. He didn't have to. He knew they were following him. He could hear their teeth clacking together like a bunch of out-of-control Halloween ornaments as they picked up speed. Pumping his arms, he ran for his life.

Riko was a dominant wolf, but a fight against four rogue wolves would only put him in the hospital, or dead. He needed to get the hell out of there, and then he could figure out what the hell he wanted to do. If anything. Maybe he'd just say "fuck it" and go home. Leave his father's body to whatever kind of funeral these idiots wanted to give him.

Riko took the corner too fast, and his boot slid on a patch of moss on the ground. He landed hard on one knee, cursed loudly, then got right back up and kept going. If he was in any pain, he wouldn't know it for all the adrenaline flooding his system. Up ahead through the trees, he caught glimpses of a group of humans who'd decided to be rebellious and wandered off the trail themselves. Thank fuck. They were stupid for doing so with the snow falling heavier by the hour, but Riko had never been so appreciative of the human ego that had gotten them there. All he had to do was make it to them and he'd be in the clear. Even these assholes wouldn't risk exposure to humans by attacking him in full view.

Then something else came into play. A male moose, easily six feet tall at its shoulder, raised its big head and watched him coming, big jaw moving in circles as it gnawed on sweet grass.

He waved his arms at the stupid animal. "Run! Run, you stupid thing!" But the moose stayed exactly where it was, watching the crowd of crazy running at it right up until the last minute. As Riko ran past, it let out a grunt of encouragement, and finally decided to get the fuck up out of there. Spinning on its back hooves, it took off in the opposite direction, away from the humans and the wolves.

Riko gazed after it wistfully for just a second before he took advantage of the distraction it gave him and hauled ass the rest of the way down the hill.

But as luck would have it, the sounds of the bull moose crashing through the underbrush was enough to startle the humans. As one, the group stopped talking and started power walking as quietly as they could back toward the trail. Riko almost called out after them but caught himself at the last minute. It was a small group. Smaller than he'd originally thought. If the wolves hadn't spotted them yet, he didn't want to put them in any danger.

Zigzagging through the trees, he followed them, but he still wasn't close enough. His lungs burned like hell and his head was pounding from the lack of oxygen. He didn't have time to shift. The people were too far away. No way he'd catch up to them before the wolves caught up to him.

Fuck it.

Riko skidded to a stop and bent over, bracing his hands on his knees as he tried to catch his breath.

The wolves were on him in a heartbeat, forming a circle around his out of shape ass. They paced nervously, unsure of what to do now that he'd ended the chase.

Riko kept one eye on their leader, the other on his playmates. He thought he recognized him now as one of the guys he used to play football with in school. The guy was too arrogant then, and it looked like things hadn't changed much. Hopefully, he had a little more control over his wolf these days.

Straightening up, he enjoyed the fact that he towered over them all and kept eye contact with their leader. "Stan," he greeted him.

The wolf in question snarled, baring his teeth.

"Don't tell me you don't remember me." Riko put a hand to his chest, as though the very idea pained him. "I thought we were buds." He dropped his arm back down to his side. "So stop being a douche. I'm just here to bury my father. Then I'll be out of your hair, so to speak." He grinned, but it seemed Stan still didn't share his sense of humor.

With a barked command, the other wolves pounced, taking Riko down to the ground in a tangle of fur and teeth. Although he'd tried to avoid it, it was within their rights to make a show of force. He'd expected this move. He'd also expected them to take things way too far, which is why he'd run, and that's exactly what they were doing.

He managed to keep them away from his throat, but there was nothing he could do to protect the rest of him. They chewed him up quite a bit before Riko finally rolled onto his side and curled into a ball, reached into his boot, and pulled out his knife.

Because when things got out of hand, it was also within *his* fucking rights to protect himself.

He slashed upward as he threw himself back the other way, catching one of them behind the front leg. The wolf yelped and jumped away, falling forward when he tried to stand up.

It was enough to get the other's attention off of him long enough for him to get back on his feet, the knife held out in front of him. A low growl vibrated deep in his throat, his own wolf pushing on his ribcage to get out and fight. With great effort, Riko kept him contained. Turning now would not only make him vulnerable during the change, but it would basically be declaring war. By staying human, he was relating his wish not to fight. And if this pack had any kind of honor left at all, they'd back the hell off.

If not, well... Riko eyed the four wolves, only one of whom he'd recognized. Before they'd jumped him, and if he had his axe, he might've had a chance. But now, hurt and bleeding as he was, the odds weren't in his favor.

Riko waited, trying not to show how out of breath he was, as the wolves made their decision. And all he could think of was how he should've kissed Addison when he'd had the chance.

The wolves herded Riko back the way they'd came, and he went along with them without a fight. Now that the posturing was over, they could get down to the business of why he'd come back.

His left leg was killing him, and from the way his jeans stuck to his calf and the acrid scent of copper in his nose, he'd say he was bleeding quite a bit. One of these beasts had gotten a good chomp on his thigh, though from what he could tell, that bite was the worst of his injuries. Lucky for him it was winter, and he was wearing a coat of a decent thickness that protected the rest of him just enough that he wasn't bleeding out before his body had time to heal itself. Not a common occurrence for a shifter, but not unheard of, either.

When they finally made it back to the cave where the pack holed up when they got tired of playing human in town, the large wolf shifted back to his skin as the others

—some in skin and some in fur—gathered around to see what all the commotion was about. A few of the females he kinda sorta recognized looked happy to see him. Some of the males not so much.

Riko winked at a blonde he vaguely remembered while Stan found his jeans and sweater, more to piss off the male hovering behind her than anything else, and grinned when she frowned at the guy's growl of displeasure. It appeared that relationship was a little one sided.

"What the fuck are you doing here, Riko?"

Riko didn't respond, staring at Stan, the guy who had been an asshole in school, and apparently still was.

"Riko Silvano, is that really you?" the blonde asked, her smile widening.

Riko gave her a nod but refrained from winking at her again. Barely. It wasn't that he had any real interest in her, he just loved to stir the pot.

"You disappear without a trace for twenty years, abandon your pack, leave your family, only to come back now?" Stan asked. "When your old man is dead?" One side of his upper lip lifted in a show of disgust. "You have no friends here anymore, Silvano."

Taking a deep breath, Riko took a few seconds to tame his wolf. He didn't like the way Stan was talking to him, when Riko was the more dominant wolf. But now was not the time to get into that. "Why the hell else would I have come back here?" he said.

Stan, who it seemed was his father's second in command, gave him a once over. Riko could tell he hadn't officially become alpha yet, but he desperately wanted to. "Look," he told him. "I'm just here to bury my old man. Pay my respects. And then I'm going back to Oklahoma."

"Does your alpha even know where you are? Assuming you have a new pack, that is." His tone reeked of superiority.

"He does." Riko kept his reply simple. It told the other wolves all they needed to know—his location was known and there would be hell to pay if he didn't come back. Especially since this wasn't just him encroaching on another pack's territory for no reason. He was here to mourn a family member, and so he was guaranteed to be able to come and go without harm. It was the general rule among packs. Breaking that rule brought shame and disrespect upon the pack that did so.

Stan walked closer to him, his nostrils flaring, and Riko knew he was taking his scent. As if there was any doubt whose kid he is. He'd been the spitting image of his father from the day he was born.

"You reek of human," he announced loudly, even though it wasn't necessary. They could all hear him just fine. "Actually, one human in particular." Indicating for one of the other wolves to come closer, Stan ordered him to sniff. "Am I right?" he asked.

The other wolf gave a nod.

"I see you haven't changed," he told Riko with disgust. "You just get back into town and the first thing you do is go sniffing around Addison's skirts. Just like in high school."

"Well, technically, she wasn't wearing a skirt. She was wearing jeans." Riko grinned, remembering how good she looked in them.

"This is why you'll never be the alpha," Stan told him. "Rolling around in the dirt with humans makes you no better than they are. And it dilutes our bloodline. Which is why mating with them is not allowed. The next thing you know, there'll be none of us left."

Riko rolled his eyes. "I wasn't rolling around with anyone. We just kind of bumped into each other...so to speak."

"That woman is not a friend of the pack—"

"Nor do I intend her to be," Riko told him. "I'm not even a member of this pack, and I sure as hell don't intend to become one again, so I don't even know why you're getting your panties in a wad about it."

A few of the wolves took a step closer, baring their teeth with a growl. Riko heaved a sigh. "Look man, I was just saying hi. That's it." He paused. "And trying to get myself a little dinner."

At that, Stan crossed his arms over his chest and barked out a laugh with no humor, as though that was the most ridiculous thing he'd ever heard. "You were trying to get her cow."

It was Riko's turn to laugh. "Like you and your lapdogs here never tried doing the same exact fucking thing," Riko told him. He suddenly had an interesting thought. Leaning his weight on his good leg, he mimicked Stan's pose, crossing his arms over his chest and frowning as though deep in thought. "How many years have you been trying to catch that cow now?" he asked him. "And you still haven't managed to do it?"

That took him down a notch. "It's complicated," Stan told him with a scowl.

"Complicated, my ass. It's a fucking cow."

"I don't see you hauling' a side of beef on your back."

"I was intercepted by a beautiful woman. The one you so rudely used your sniffer dogs here to detect." No need to admit just *how* he was thrown off the hunt.

Riko started to get uncomfortable as Stan stared at him for a long moment. And then something resembling a genuine smile broke out across his face. "You got caught up in one of her traps." And he started laughing. The wolves surrounding him quickly caught on and howled with mirth, the sound echoing through the tall trees.

Riko waited until they'd quieted down, and then shrugged nonchalantly. "It's not the first time a pretty girl tried to trap me," he joked. "But as you can see," he spread out his arms to the sides, "here I am. Still a lone wolf."

"Yeah well, maybe next time she'll let the bear snack on you." Stan chuckled at his own joke, but he was the only one this time. Then he just stood there for a long time, staring at Riko, and he could tell he didn't know what to do with him. He would bet his good leg the douche was debating whether to follow protocol or make a big show of sending him on his way, maybe missing a few body parts, just to prove to himself and everyone else what a badass he was.

This guy doesn't have the teeth to be alpha if he can't even decide what to do with an old "friend" who only came back for a funeral. But that wasn't Riko's problem. "Look," he finally said. "Are you gonna do something here? Or are we just gonna hang out and enjoy the snow? Maybe make some snow angels? Build a snowman?" The flakes were getting bigger and coming down harder. If Stan kept it up with his bullshit it'd be up to his knees before he let them all leave. "How about we stop with the peacocking and you can let me know if you're gonna let me bury my father, or if you're gonna toss me out of this territory on my ass."

He purposefully neglected saying "your territory", because it wasn't his yet, much as Stan appeared to like to strut around and bark orders as though it were. Especially now that Riko was back. Not because he was blood of the previous alpha, but because he was the more dominant wolf. In a normal pack, if he wanted the position of alpha, Riko would have to fight any others who wanted to make a run for it until he was the last one standing, proving his strength and his dominance over the other wolves. But somehow, he knew if he threw his hat in the ring here, it wouldn't be a respectful fight, one wolf at a time. It would be a free for all, and the odds were he wouldn't make it out alive.

Good thing he had no desire whatsoever to stay.

Stan narrowed his eyes, glancing around at the others. Riko could tell he wasn't happy about being called out in front of the others, but at least Stan had enough brain cells to realize there wasn't a damn thing he could do about it without proving Riko to be correct.

"You can stay," he finally said. "Funeral's the day after tomorrow. We're preparing the body now." He turned his head and lifted his chin toward the interior of the cave. "However, you need to find someplace to bunk down in town, you're not staying with the pack."

"And why the hell not?" Riko asked him. It wasn't that he wanted to stay with them, he would've turned him down if Stan had offered. But it was the normal protocol.

"Because I don't fucking trust you," Stan said. "You're not reliable. You left this pack first chance you got and never looked back until now. You could be using your father's death as a ruse to pull something over on us."

In spite of himself, Riko was a tad bit insulted. "That's a shitty way to treat a guest," he told him. "And you can be sure my alpha's gonna hear about it."

"From what I hear," Stan said, "Keegan has his hands plenty full dealing with the Texas *and* Oklahoma backs combined. Especially now that he stopped his rodeo. I doubt he'll care that you weren't offered a soft bed to sleep in."

This is probably true, Riko thought to himself. But still, it's just rude. "I'll be back the day after tomorrow," he told him, and turned to leave.

"Don't you want to see your father's body?" Stan douchebag asked.

Riko looked back over his shoulder, and for the first time, the smirk left his face. "No. I really don't."

Turning to leave, he found his way blocked by the other wolves. Riko spread his hands to the sides and lifted one eyebrow, a low growl of warning deep in his throat. He'd had enough of the games. Eventually the pack parted, much like the Red Sea, and let him go.

CHAPTER 5

$\mathcal{A}$ddison sat at the end of the bar away from everyone else and sipped her house red. The place was a dive. An old garage one of the guys she'd known since birth had turned into a small-town bar, aptly named "Greg's Bar." The interior consisted of a bar made of recycled wood, a pool table that had seen better days, a dozen or so tables with mismatched chairs, and an actual jukebox that worked. Sometimes. But it was her favorite place to drink. Mostly because there were only about five other people besides her who came there on the regular, and after they said hello, they left her alone.

Except for tonight. Tonight, Carl Covey—the greatest high school football legend in her town—had decided, once again, to make a play for the one girl who'd never noticed him...

Because she was too busy following Riko through the halls.

Addison stared at the reflection of the two of them in the mirror behind the bar. She had to admit, Carl still looked pretty good, and they complimented each other well. Hell, he was even kinda funny.

She laughed at his latest story about one of the customers at the supply store he'd inherited from his parents and felt his large hand on her back.

"How is it?" Carl asked, pointing to her glass. "Greg told me it was a new shipment, a merlot this time."

Honestly, she could've been drinking bear piss and she wouldn't have even noticed. "It's good," she told him, mustering up a smile. "How's Joyce?"

As he launched into a play-by-play of why he wasn't dating his first love anymore, Addison tuned him out. It's not that she didn't care, Joyce had been one of her nicer friends all through school, and Addison knew she still had it bad for her high school sweetheart, which was why she'd never encouraged him. It was just that right now, she had other things on her mind.

Well, just one other thing. Riko Silvano.

Why, oh *why*, did he have to come back? Right when she'd finally stopped thinking about him? Well, okay, she thought about him sometimes. Once in a while. Okay, maybe a few times a week. But it's not like she could control what she dreamed about. Still, that didn't mean she wanted him back in her life. Not even for just a few days. She was sorry his dad had passed, she really was, but couldn't he have just driven into town using a car like a normal person instead of tromping through the woods and right into her trap? You know, gotten a room at the Riverside Inn Hotel just outside of town. Laid low. Gone to the cemetery and then hightailed it back to wherever the hell he'd come from without her ever having to lay eyes on his handsome face.

As though she'd conjured him up by thinking about him, Riko walked into the bar. Addison watched him in the mirror, Carl all but forgotten beside her even though he was currently playing with the ends of her hair. But Riko didn't miss what was happening, and she felt a thrill rush through her as Riko zeroed in on the two of him, his eyes going from Carl standing so close to her to where his hand lay on her back.

She saw Riko's fists clench at his sides and would swear his eyes flashed yellow before he took a visible breath and started toward them. Addison watched him come, curious if he was going to lay Carl out on the floor or just pick her up and throw her over his shoulder. Either option seemed to be a viable one going by the look on his face.

But Riko surprised her, appearing on the empty stool on the other side of her. "Hey. Anyone sitting here?"

Addison closed her eyes as the rumble of his deep voice sent chills over her skin. "Yeah. What's left of my pride," she mumbled.

"Your what?" he asked as he made himself comfortable and flagged down Greg to bring him a beer.

"Nothing," she told him. "What are you doing here? Are you following me or what?"

Riko thanked Greg for his beer and told him to start a tab. "Not at all. I was just looking for a place to wind down. Plus, I'm staying at that cabin rental right across the street." He took a long pull from his bottle and set it on the bar.

Addison realized he hadn't looked straight at her once since he'd sat down. "Are you okay?"

"I'm good." He took another drink, finishing off two-thirds of his beer, and raised his hand to Greg to get him another.

Addison watched him chug down his second bottle. Carl asked her something, she couldn't have said what, and when she didn't respond, he wandered over to the closest table to talk to someone else. Addison didn't care. Her entire focus was on Riko, the same as it had always been. She wanted to ask him what was bothering him, but she bit her tongue. Dammit, she was not going to fall back into being the stupid, naive girl she was in high school. That lost and lonely girl, despite what people saw on the outside. An expert on presenting the façade she wanted them to see. A façade no one had seen through except for one beautiful boy, who had grown into this sexy man sitting beside her.

Not only had he seen through it, he'd smashed it open to release the real Addison inside. He'd gotten under her skin. Gotten to know her. He'd made her feel safe. Like she could be herself. She'd never had to put on a show or pretend to be someone she wasn't around him. When everyone else had wandered off to do their own thing after high school and no longer needed her popularity, Riko had been there. He'd become her best friend, and eventually her lover.

And then he'd left without so much as a goodbye.

As she watched him in the mirror, she half expected him to make some snide remark about her being there with Carl. Or worse, the way Riko was keeping an eye on him.

"It killed me to leave you, you know," he said quietly.

His eyes met hers in the mirror, and Addison felt her face heat for the eight hundredth time since he'd come back into town. God, did he read minds now? She cleared her throat with her wine. "What?"

Riko finally turned his head and looked straight at her. The intensity with which he stared at her caught her off guard, and she felt her heart catch in her chest. "I didn't want to leave you, Addi. But at the time, I didn't see any other way."

Staring into his gorgeous brown eyes, the bar, the music, the laughter, it all faded away. It seemed to take forever for her heart to beat again.

. . .

Riko watched as Addison tried to decide whether or not to believe him, her emotions flashing across her face like an old film reel before they finally settled back into the picture of insufferable impatience she'd worn since she'd found him dangling in her net. The film had snapped, and a blank screen took its place.

"I don't believe you." Then she spun on her stool, hopped down, and walked away.

Distracted by the full shape of her ass, perfectly outlined in her worn jeans, he almost let her leave just so he could watch her walk away. Had she always had such a fine ass? He couldn't remember.

He finished his beer real quick and caught up to her just as she grabbed the handle of the door to leave.

"Addison, wait!"

She released the door handle and turned around. "You. Left. Me." She spoke each word clearly and succinctly, ignoring the curious stares from the five other people in the bar. "Without a word. So, don't come back here giving me your sob story about how hard it was for you, Riko."

He could see it clearly now, how much he'd hurt her. It surprised him a bit. The last time he'd seen her, Addi was talking about going off to cosmetology school once she'd saved up a little money from her waitressing job. Not once had she mentioned him or their relationship. One

Riko had risked—and eventually lost—his place in the pack for. "Are you still waiting tables?"

She frowned at him. "What? No. I work at the bank."

"That's a step up, at least. What happened to beauty school?"

"Riko—"

No. He couldn't let her leave. Not yet. Seeing her again... he knew it would be hard. But he hadn't expected *this*. "Addi, just...come talk to me. I'm right across the street. I have," he racked his brain, trying to remember what was in his kitchen, "nothing at all to offer you, but maybe Greg here will let us buy a bottle from him. What do you say?" He gave her his most winning smile.

Instead of melting like a normal woman, she stalked closer, getting right up in his face, though she had to stand on her toes and tilt her head way back to do it. "I'm not going anywhere with you until you tell me why you— the only person in the world who ever gave a shit about me—up and left me without even leaving me a note. Was it all just a game for you? Why didn't you ever come for me? Why did you leave me here, in this shit town, alone, to survive all on my own?" His chest ached as her eyes got all shiny. "Tell me *why*, Riko!"

Riko let her scream at him. He understood how much she was hurting, because so was he. "Addison, come back to the house with me."

"Fuck that." She backed away a few steps. "I'm not falling for you again, Riko. Not when I've been stuck here...*alone*...all of this time with nothing but my father and fucking Mistletoe to keep me company. Not when you're just going to leave me again as soon as your father is in the ground."

Somebody tried to open the door and Riko moved out of the way, pulling Addison with him. "What are you talking about? You have tons of friends."

She shook her head slowly. "No. I don't. I didn't. I had a bunch of fake bitches who only cared about me because I could get them on my prom court just for being seen with me on a daily basis."

Riko tried to catch her eye, but she wouldn't look at him. He ran a hand over his hair, an unconscious gesture of frustration. "Addi, I'm so sorry. I just assumed..." *That I didn't mean as much to you as you did to me, and you wouldn't miss me.*

Addison stared up at him, deadpan. "Well, you assumed wrong." Reaching into her front pocket, she pulled out her car keys. Her composure crumbled as the tears in her eyes overflowed to streak down her cheeks, and she ran out the door.

Riko sighed heavily. "Well, that went better than I expected." He should let her go. Addi was human. He was a shifter. And the more he hung around with her, the greater the risk that he'd be exposing her to that side of himself. The main reason shifters were still around was because they kept their identity secret from humans. He'd only be putting her in danger if he chased after her. The Colorado pack was strict about taking out anything and anyone they deemed a threat. And he wouldn't be here to protect her.

Pushing the door open, he followed her outside.

CHAPTER 6

Addison blinked back tears as she left the bar and rushed over to her car. Stopping for a minute to get herself together, she spotted Mistletoe wandering between houses across from the bar. She was probably finally heading home to bed down for the night. The cow was old, and probably on her last year of life, but Addison just couldn't bring herself to have her slaughtered.

He obviously didn't remember it, but Riko had helped her birth that damn cow.

It was Christmas Eve night of their senior year of high school. One of their breeding cows had gotten through the fence, as she did at least once a week, and Addison had gone out on her quad to try to find her and chase her back to the barn. More because she liked to ride the quad than because she cared about the cow.

She'd found the mom-to-be way back in the fields behind the gas station that was the last stop out of town. She was lying on her side in the tall grass, and when Addison walked up to her, she could see why.

Two skinny legs and a nose were sticking out of the birth canal. However, the baby appeared to be stuck.

Not knowing what else to do, Addison wiped her hands on her jeans and squatted down to help her, but even after a good few minutes of the cow pushing and Addison pulling, the calf wouldn't budge.

And that was when Riko had shown up out of nowhere wearing nothing but a pair of Levi's and a flannel shirt, despite the fact that it was twenty-seven degrees outside. He'd taken one look at the situation and knelt down behind the cow and muscled that calf out.

It was the first time Addison had seen him outside of school. The first time they'd talked. The first time they'd laughed together.

As it began to snow, Addison had named the calf Mistletoe...

"Addi! Wait!"

Furiously, Addison wiped the tears from her face. Her fingers were like ice just from the little bit of time she'd been standing there. All she wanted was to get the hell home and into a hot bath and a bottle of wine—not necessarily in that order—where she could be miserable and alone. Just like the last twenty years.

As she fumbled with her keys and tried to unlock her car, Riko's hand wrapped around her wrist.

"Don't go."

Addison stilled, but wouldn't face him. She couldn't. She didn't want him to see what a wreck she really was because of him.

"Don't go, Addi. Stay here with me for a while."

She closed her eyes. "Why?" she choked out. When he didn't respond, she sniffed and lifted her chin, finally turning to look up at him.

Riko stared down at her, his eyes bright with all of the pain she was feeling. There wasn't an ounce of ego shining there. Only apologies he'd never spoken and the same sense of loneliness she thought she'd learned to live with. "Don't go," was all he said.

"Oh, God," she whispered. Addison could feel her resolve weakening at an alarming rate. It was easy to push him away when he was being egotistical, smirky Riko. But she had no defense at all against this Riko, who was all broken and sincere and tugged at her heartstrings.

"Please." He smiled at her. A real smile that was shy and unsure, not the smirk he usually gave her. "Don't go. Stay with me, Addi."

"For how long?" she asked softly. "For tonight? A week? What?"

He touched her face with his fingertips. His hands were warm, and it brought back forgotten memories of how warm his bare skin was everywhere.

"I don't know. I just know that against my better judgement, I can't stand to watch you leave right now"— the muscles in his jaw clenched and released—"and I want you to stay with me."

She opened her mouth to tell him no. To tell him she wanted to go home, even though it was a lie. But before she could say anything, he ducked his head and his mouth was moving on hers. Timidly at first, just a brush of his lips, and then with more urgency when she didn't push him away. She gasped when he nipped her bottom lip, and Riko took the opportunity to go deeper. His arms tightened around her as his tongue teased hers, and he kissed her with all of the desperation she was trying so hard to keep inside.

But she couldn't. With a moan, she rose up onto her tiptoes and wrapped her arms around his shoulders even as a tear fell silently down her cheek. She'd forgotten how good he felt. How perfectly she fit against him.

"Don't cry," he whispered as he kissed away the moisture on her cheeks. "It's okay, Addi. It'll be okay."

She wasn't so sure about that, but she didn't say anything when he took her face between his large hands and searched her eyes for the answer to his unspoken question. Tears welling in her eyes again until his handsome face was nothing but a blur, she nodded. She needed this. She needed him. And she would take the heartbreak that would come later when he left her again just to have this night with the man she'd loved since she was a teenager.

The funny thing was, he looked as broken up about it all as she felt. But it made no sense. Why would he have left and caused them both to be so miserable if he wanted to be with her, too?

She had no time to ask him as he took her hand and hurried her across the street to the cabin he was renting. It was just another reminder that he wasn't there to stay. Addison looked up into the dark sky as the flurries that had teased them all day began to fall in fat flakes all around her, an omen of what was to come.

He pulled her into the cabin and shut the door behind them. A light was on over the stove, and Addison barely had time to catch an overall glimpse of dark wood and brown leather decor before she was pushed up against the closed door and Riko was taking her coat off and then his own. Addison moaned as he caught her lips with his again. He tasted like dark beer and smelled like the outdoors and spice. She felt tiny in his strong arms. Fragile. And yet oh so powerful as she made him whimper in the back of his throat just by sliding her hand beneath his shirt to the hot skin beneath. Her hand stilled as she felt the muscles tense beneath it.

She just needed a moment. Just a moment…

"Please don't tell me to stop," Riko whispered.

Addison shook her head. "No, I don't want you to stop. I just forgot—"

He lifted his head just enough to stare down at her. "What?"

But she only shook her head again. There was no way to explain how overwhelming this man was. Sex with him wasn't just a pleasurable pastime. If she gave herself to him, he would possess her completely. Own her. Mind, body, and soul. There would be nothing else but Riko and what he was doing to her when she was with him.

She just needed a moment.

"Addi?"

She pulled his mouth back down to hers. She didn't want to talk. She didn't want to think. She just wanted to feel Riko on top of her. Wanted to forget what would come after.

He growled deep in his throat and chill bumps broke out across her skin. Riko undressed her slowly, and only stopped kissing her long enough to stare with wonder at each new part of her body he revealed before his hands were exploring her curves and his mouth was commanding hers again.

Addison's fingers trembled as she tried to undo the buttons of his shirt. Finally, she gave up and just gave it a yank. Buttons clattered to the floor and she got it halfway off his broad shoulders before he bent down and lifted her into his strong arms. Her legs wrapped around his hips as he carried her across the room and laid her carefully on his bed.

Riko never took his eyes from her as he rid himself of his boots, jeans, and shirt, dropping them on the floor. Addison watched, much as he had, as he revealed each powerful arm, her eyes traveling down over flat, rippling abs to that "V" at his hips right above the waistband of his jeans. And when he pushed those jeans down, her insides clenched with anticipation. It'd been so long since she'd been with anyone, and none of them compared to this man.

Instead of joining her on the bed, he grabbed her calves and pulled her down to the edge. Addison was about to sit up when he dropped to his knees between her legs. As he pushed her thighs apart, she fell back with a helpless sound, her fingers gripping the patchwork quilt beneath her. And when he kissed her hipbone, then the crease between her leg and her sex, she hung on for dear life.

Riko growled low as he nosed the soft curls covering her folds. She heard him inhale deep just before the tip of his tongue touched her clit.

Addison lifted her hips shamelessly, seeking more of his mouth. "Please, Riko." His name ended on a moan as he gave her what she begged for, his tongue licking her slit from back to front before finding that spot that drove her mad. An aching heaviness began in her womb, desire ebbing and flowing until she was panting and whimpering with need.

Wrapping his arms around her legs, he pulled her closer to his mouth until she wondered if he was going to devour her completely. The pleasure low in her stomach became nearly painful, hovering on the precipice for a long moment before it rushed over the edge in great pulses of pleasure.

Riko moaned as he tasted her release, his tongue penetrating her over and over. Then he nipped her thigh and rose over her. Addison had no time to recover before his teeth were grazing her nipples, first one then the other, and she felt the head of his cock nudging her entrance.

"I have to be inside you," he told her through gritted teeth.

Addison hung on tight to his shoulders as he pushed his way in. He was long and hard and thick, and she cried out at the intensity of feeling him so deep inside of her.

"Gods, Addi," he groaned, his big body shuddering in her arms.

The gods aren't going to help us, she thought. Then she gripped his hips as he started to move over her. He didn't go slow. Didn't take his time. He was a man possessed, fucking her hard and fast, her name a prayer in her ear more powerful than anything she'd ever heard at church as he took over her body until she had no control anymore. Until all she knew was Riko—his mouth, his teeth, his hands. He was everywhere. Touching her. Whispering things in her ear that made her blush even though his cock was inside of her. Until she thought she couldn't take it because it was all too much, only to have him demand more from her.

Holding himself on one elbow, he slid his other hand beneath her ass, lifting her off the bed and sinking even deeper inside of her. Addison cried out his name as another orgasm crashed over her, her body pulsing around him as he thrust deep, crying out her name and sinking his teeth into the muscle between her neck and shoulder as he held her tight against him.

And when he rolled to the side and pulled her to his chest, he smoothed her hair down her back as she burst into tears, overwhelmed with emotions she couldn't even name.

"It's okay," he told her again. "It'll be okay, Addi."

No. No it wouldn't.

CHAPTER 7

Riko woke with a jerk, his heart pounding so hard he thought it was about to explode. Sitting up, he placed one hand on his chest in a vain attempt to keep it in there. He kept his breathing quiet, searching the dimly lit room for whatever it was that had woken him.

Addi was by the door, fully dressed, pulling on her boots.

"Where are you going?" The words came out harsher than he intended.

She glanced over at him as she put her coat on, and for a second he thought she was going to leave without answering him. But then she stilled, staring at the floor for a long moment before she turned toward him. Her eyes ran over his bare torso, almost like she was trying to commit him to memory, and then she said simply, "Home."

He jumped out of bed and searched for his jeans, a sense of urgency he couldn't explain driving him. It's not like he didn't know where to find her. "Hang on. I'll walk you to your car."

She waved him off. "That's not necessary, Riko. It's right across the street."

Her voice was dispassionate. Her expression completely blank. She'd barely left his bed and she was already shutting him out.

And maybe she was right. He had nothing to offer her. Fuck, she didn't even know what he really was. Going any farther with this would only lead to another twenty years of loneliness and anger and pain for both of them. Maybe worse if his old man's pack caught a whiff of what had happened here tonight. It was bad enough they already had her in their sights just because he'd seen her first when he'd gotten into town.

His wolf paced restlessly beneath his skin, already mourning her loss.

No. No. He couldn't just let her leave like this. Riko yanked up his pants and threw his hands out in front of him as she went for the door. "I said just hang on! Okay? Just...just wait a minute. One damn minute." He had a horrible premonition that if he let her walk out that door, he would never see her again. Which was stupid. It was a small town. Tiny, really. Where would she hide?

Addison stared at him, unmoving.

"I'm sorry." He sighed and grabbed his boots, then looked around for his shirt. "I didn't mean to snap at you, Addi. Just wait for me. Please." A strong sense of *déjà vu* went through him. Words he'd wanted to say so many times all those years ago, but never could.

"Okay," she said quietly.

When he had himself as put together as he was gonna get, he joined her at the door. He put his hand on the knob but didn't open it. "Are you dating him?" Riko would slap himself if it wouldn't make him look like more of a fool than he already was. He didn't know where that had suddenly come from. Well, he did. He just hadn't planned on asking.

The mask fell from Addison's face as she looked up at him in confusion. "Who?"

"Carl," Riko could barely unclench his jaw enough to get the name out.

"*Carl?*" She made a noise that was something between a laugh and a sound of disgust. "Why would I be sleeping with you if I was dating Carl? Or anyone, for that matter?"

She was telling the truth. He'd always known when she tried to lie to him because she was horrible at it.

"He wants to fuck you." *For fuck's sake, man. Shut your damn mouth.*

"So what?" He noticed she didn't try to deny it. "And seriously, Riko. What right do you have to ask me that?"

Her face was flushed, her eyes shooting daggers, and she was leaning forward on her hips. Between one second and the next, the dam had broke. That was good. He could handle pissed off Addi. Sad Addi. Indignant Addi. Whatever. He didn't care. At least she was letting him in.

"Like, really?" she continued, her voice rising with every word. "You've been gone. GONE, Riko. I haven't seen you in twenty years. And you just come waltzing back here acting like you've never left. I'm thirty-nine fucking years old—"

"Thirty-eight."

"—and I'm too fucking old for this shit!"

"You're beautiful."

"And you can't just come back here, fuck me like... like...*that*"—she pointed at the bed—"and then leave again. Leave *me* again. Which is exactly what you're going to do. And don't lie to me and tell me you're not. What the hell is wrong with you?"

That was a really good question. And he knew the answer. He was a shifter with abandonment issues. His mother had died, and his father never cared enough to even ask where he was going or if he'd be back when he'd told him he was leaving. But he couldn't tell her that.

"Come with me." The words were out of his mouth before he realized what he was about to say.

Her mouth snapped shut and she took a step back. "What?"

Riko didn't know what he was doing. There was no way this would work. She was human. She didn't know about his kind. And yeah, they'd had some fun back in the day —and tonight—but he'd always known it could never be anything long term. It wasn't safe for either of them. But the sight of her sitting there with some other dude's arm around her...making her laugh...*touching* her...

"Come with me when I leave, Addi."

She stared at him like he'd grown horns. "No." Her voice and posture were calm. Too calm. "Now, please move so I can go home." Dropping her eyes to somewhere in the middle of his chest, she waited.

Riko wasn't sure what to make of Addison's blasé reaction to his comment. Granted, he was only half serious when he'd said it. Right?

Right??

Okay. Maybe seventy—no, sixty—all right, ninety percent —serious. But now that he'd said it, he realized he'd meant it. One hundred and fifty percent. But one look at her stunned face (had she always had those adorable freckles across the top of her nose?) and it made him wonder how she would react when she found out he was a shifter.

There was only way to find out. "Addi—"

Her eyes flew to his in a panic and she slapped one hand over his mouth. "Stop. Just…stop. I just want to go home." Tears filled her eyes and spilled onto her cheeks.

Riko reached up and gently removed her hand. He wanted to take back what he'd said. And in the same breath he wanted to put her in his truck and take her back to Oklahoma with him. He had no idea how his alpha would react if he brought her home with him, or whether she'd be able to stay with the pack or not. But there was one thing he'd realized tonight—he couldn't leave here without her again. It had nearly killed him the first time. And by the way she'd responded to him since he'd come back—both in bed and out—he'd bet Addi wanted to be with him, too. She was just mad about the last twenty years, was all. And she had every right to be.

He'd known back in high school that this woman would haunt him. His heart had literally stopped the first time he'd seen her, and he'd tried to stay away from her. He really, really had. But when he'd come across her that winter night he was out hunting in his wolf form and found her trying to birth that calf, the scent of blood and amniotic fluid burning his nose and making his mouth water, his first instinct hadn't been to take advantage of the weakened animal.

It had been not to hurt Addison.

So, despite the temptation of the distressed cow, he'd shifted back, found his clothes, and ran over to help her pull the calf out. Addi had named her Mistletoe.

A light flicked on in Riko's brain. "The cow..."

Addison shoved him out of the way, and he let her, too dumbfounded he hadn't remembered that little piece of history until just now. *That* was why she wouldn't let him have steak for dinner. Mistletoe was...Mistletoe!

"I'm out of here," she said in a voice thick with tears as she yanked the door open. "And don't you dare touch my damn cow!"

Riko ran out after her, the only thought running through his head being that he couldn't let her leave. Not like this. And in so doing he let his guard down. Forgot to be aware of his surroundings. Let himself feel too secure in this place he both loved and hated, but where he'd always felt at home. It wasn't until he heard the rippling effect of multiple wolves growling a warning that he realized his mistake.

Addison suddenly stopped where she was in the middle of the street and whipped back around to look at Riko, her eyes wide with fear and her quick breaths a cloud in the cold air.

Four wolves edged out onto the road, their paws completely silent in the snow that now covered everything like a scene from a nostalgic postcard. They surrounded her, teeth bared and hackles up. As Riko watched, the darkest one sank down onto his haunches, preparing to launch himself at her. He knew those wolves...

After that, the rest was a blur.

Fury roared through Riko such as he'd never felt before, followed by the tearing of flesh and cracking of bone as the shift tore through him fast and hard, the pain blinding. He didn't even have time to shake it off before he was charging the attacking wolf, knocking him off his paws and sinking his teeth into his throat, Addi's muffled scream in his ears.

Tossing the wolf's limp body to the ground, he planted himself in front of Addison, who stood with both hands covering her mouth, and faced off with the other three wolves. Running completely on animal instinct now, Riko growled deep in his throat. Head down, teeth bared in a snarl, tail up and hackles raised, he stared them down.

They didn't back off right away. But neither did they attack.

Riko heard Addison whimper in fear behind him right before her footstep crunched in the snow. Without taking his eyes from the other wolves, he turned his head and snapped his teeth at her. She froze where she was, and he returned his full focus back to the ones who dared to threaten her.

Slowly, one by one, heads lowered, soon followed by tails and bodies as they whined their acceptance of his dominance.

Riko lifted his head and backed up a few steps, giving them permission to leave. But it wasn't until he was sure they were gone that he relaxed his stance and turned to check on Addison. Luckily, this all went down on the edge of town, and it was late enough now that everyone was either shitfaced drunk or asleep. A few wolf howls and growls weren't enough to get most folks out of their warm beds in this part of the country.

Addison was staring at him in horror, her eyes going back and forth from his torn clothes lying in the road, back to him, and then back to his clothes again, as though she was trying to convince herself of what she'd just seen with her own eyes. She started backing away and when Riko took a step forward to reassure her, she turned and ran to her car.

His first instinct was to chase her, but he knew that would only frighten her more. So with no small amount of effort, he held himself back, watching as she tried to unlock her car with shaking hands. It took her a minute, but eventually she got it, yanked the car door open, and threw herself inside before she slammed it shut and locked it, part of her coat hanging outside. A few seconds later, she was peeling out of the parking lot.

Riko followed her, loping silently through the empty streets and staying out of the glow of what few streetlamps there were between there and her house. When she arrived home, he crept as close as he dared without her seeing him. He didn't want to invade her space, he just wanted to make sure she made it into the house and that her and her dad were safe.

His heart shattered in his chest listening to her sobs as she ran into the house. He wanted so bad to talk to her, but tonight he'd leave her be. Let her process everything. However, his furry ass was camping outside her house just to make sure those assholes didn't come back.

Because at some point the wolves *would* be back, and they'll be bringing friends. There's no way in hell they planned to let her live now. Not knowing what she knows.

By shifting right in front of her, Riko had just signed her death warrant.

CHAPTER 8

When the pale light of the winter sun crept through her window, Addison rolled out of bed and grabbed her heaviest robe. It was an ugly peach thing from a discount store, but she'd been shivering all night, unable to stop, and the robe was warm.

Around three, she'd gotten up and walked over to the window, scared she'd find a pack of giant wolves surrounding her house. But there'd only been one.

Riko.

She'd gotten back into bed, comforted somehow that he was there, standing guard. But now she half wondered if she'd dreamt the whole thing. She didn't bother to look at her reflection in the bathroom mirror as she stuck her hair in a messy bun on top of her head and brushed her teeth. She didn't have to. She could well imagine what she looked like after not sleeping all night. Addison spit into the sink, rinsed her toothbrush and put it back into the holder, moving on autopilot. How could she dream if she hadn't slept?

Ugh. It was too much to wrap her mind around. She wouldn't believe what Riko had done at all if she hadn't seen it happen with her own eyes. And she couldn't even blame it on alcohol, though she wished she could. At least then she could write it off as being drunk and seeing things.

But she knew exactly what had happened last night. She'd seen a guy she'd known since high school burst out of his skin and turn into a wolf. A beautiful wolf. A wolf that was a combination of man and wolf, with huge muscles and intelligent eyes. But a wolf, nonetheless. With teeth and fur and a long, bushy tail.

What the actual fuck?

"Coffee. I need coffee," she muttered to herself.

Out in the kitchen, she filled the one cup coffeemaker with water and dropped a pod inside. Sticking her favorite cup underneath the drip, she hit the button for the largest cup, then walked over to the window above the sink while she waited.

Riko sat on the old porch swing, back in his...what the hell did she call it? Human form? He'd brushed the snow aside and rocked slowly back and forth, wearing only his usual attire of jeans, boots, and a red and black plaid flannel shirt. She wondered how he never got cold.

As though he sensed her looking at him, Riko turned his head and saw her, then lifted his hand in a halfhearted wave. He made no move to come to her door. He just sat there, watching her.

Addison didn't respond. She didn't know what to say or how to act around him now. Instead, she got her coffee, added cream and a little sugar, and sat down at the kitchen table, hoping he would just go away. Wrapping her icy hands around the warm cup, she took a sip, the replay from the night before swirling around in her head, stopping once in a while to focus on a particular image before speeding up again.

She wasn't sure how long she sat there before she heard the creak of the storm door open. A second later, Riko appeared in the archway leading into the kitchen, much as he had the first night he'd come back. Only this time, the tension in her stomach was for a completely different reason.

"Hey," he said softly.

"Get out of my kitchen," she responded, but there was no heat behind her words this time.

He stayed where he was. "I thought you might have some questions."

Oh, she definitely had questions. She had tons of questions. So many she didn't even know where to start.

"You don't have to be scared of me, Addi. I'd never, ever, hurt you."

Lies. He'd hurt her more than he could ever imagine twenty years ago. And he was about to hurt her again. But was she scared? Looking down at her hands, she realized they were shaking and gripped her cup harder.

"That's a God-awful robe you're wearing, by the way."

She looked up at him then. He was smirking at her. Taking another sip of her coffee, she lowered her eyes again. He was trying to make everything normal. But nothing would ever be normal between them again.

"Can I sit down?" he asked.

When she didn't respond, he helped himself to the chair beside her. She thought maybe she should ask if he wanted some coffee, but she couldn't bring herself to offer.

Leaning forward, he put his elbows on the table, careful not to invade her space. "You've gotta have questions," he said. "I'd be happy to answer them."

Yes, she did. "Um..." She paused, trying to stop her racing thoughts long enough to focus on one thing at a time. A part of her just wanted him gone, so she could pretend everything was as it was. But another part wanted him to tell her she wasn't crazy. That everything she thought she saw had really happened. "Are you the only one who can...do that?" She didn't know what to call it. Change? Shapeshift? What was the correct terminology?

Riko shook his head. "No. All of the other wolves that were there last night, they're all shifters."

Shifters. A thought suddenly occurred to her. "Do I know them?"

"Yes."

She waited for him to elaborate, but it appeared that was the only answer she was going to get. She wondered who they were, but did she really want to know?

"Addi, there's something I need to tell you."

"No. I can't, Riko." She pleaded with her eyes. "I can't go there right now. I can't..." She looked down at her coffee and took a shaky breath.

He waited until he had her attention again. "You weren't supposed to see what you did. You're not supposed to know about us. Shifters have been around here for a long time, and we only stay safe by keeping what we are a secret from the rest of you."

The rest of us humans? Is that what he meant to say?

"It was my fault. I lost it when I saw those wolves threatening you. I couldn't control the change. But you need to understand, it's not safe here for you now."

It took a second for what he was saying to penetrate her thoughts. "What do you mean?"

"Our continued existence depends on us staying below the human radar. And if something happens to put us on that radar, the pack makes sure the threat is removed." His dark eyes bored into hers, compelling her to understand what he was telling her.

Addison couldn't believe what she was hearing. A burst of laughter left her before she could stop it, and she lowered her voice so as not to wake up her father. "Are you trying to tell me that my life is in danger? My *life*?"

Riko just stared at her.

Leaning back in her seat, Addison crossed her arms over her chest and shook her head. "No. I don't believe it. Whoever this 'pack' is, they're people I've known my entire life. You can't tell me that their suddenly gonna off me because I know your little secret."

"It's a matter of survival, Addi—"

"Stop calling me that!" she hissed at him. "My *name* is Addison."

Riko pressed his lips together, but didn't argue with her. "You're not safe here anymore."

Addison shoved her chair back and stood up. "I want you to leave."

"Addi...listen to me. Please. Addison..."

But she shook her head and pointed toward the door. "I mean it, Riko. Get the hell out of here and go back to wherever the hell it is you came from, and don't ever darken my doorstep again."

He leaned back in his chair, dropping one hand to rest on his hard thigh, and looked up at her, his eyes bright with pain. "You don't mean that."

"I do," she told him. "Get out."

"What about us, Addi? What about what happened last night?" Then he quickly gave his head a shake. "Not the wolf part. The part before that."

"Before that was nothing but a lonely woman looking for something I wouldn't be running into every time I went to the store or had a glass of wine at the local bar."

He stood up then. "What if I want it to be more than that?"

Addison couldn't believe what she was hearing. Pressing both palms to her heated face, she said, "You're not even *human!*"

Riko stepped back as her words hit him. "What am I then? An animal?"

"That's sure as hell what it looked like to me." As soon as the words left her mouth, Addison wished she could take them back, but her hurt pride for the way he'd treated her all this time wouldn't let her. So, instead, she lifted her chin and stared him down, much as he had the other wolves. "And I'm not into beastiality."

He made a sound of disbelief. His mouth opened, but nothing came out, so he closed it again.

"Now. Get. Out," she gritted through her teeth, suddenly angry. How dare he think he could just walk back into her life? And on four paws, no less? What the hell did he think was going to happen here?

Riko's eyes travelled over her face and hair. "Yeah. Okay." Pushing the chair back into the table, he turned and walked out the door, pulling it shut behind him.

"I really need to start remembering to lock that thing," Addison mumbled to herself, then she promptly burst into tears. When she'd settled down to the occasional hiccup, she sniffed and went back over to the window.

That damn cow was in her front yard, pushing snow around with her nose, looking for grass to eat. As Addison watched, she lifted her big head and stared straight at her.

"Don't look at me like that," she told her.

She stood there long after Riko's truck had gone back toward town, until she heard her father's shuffling footsteps coming down the hall. "Coffee?" she asked him.

"Please," he told her, sitting down at the table with his newspaper. "Don't you have work today, Addison?"

"Not today," she told him. "It's Sunday."

"Oh, that's right."

He was quiet until she put his coffee on the table in front of him. "Was that Riko Silvano I heard out here before? The boy you had such a crush on when you were in school?"

Addison had just sat down with another coffee for herself, but at that, she looked up sharply.

Her father calmly turned the page of the paper and picked up his coffee cup, blowing on it before he took a sip.

She stared at his gray head, noticing how the hair was thinning at his temples. "No," she told him. "He's not the same boy I liked back then. He's completely different."

"Ah, honey. We're all different now than we were twenty years ago. Maybe you should cut him a little slack. Don't make the boy grovel."

Picking up her cup, Addison inhaled the rich smell of the coffee, letting it ground her. Riko Silvano couldn't get out of town fast enough for her.

Riko left Addison's house, but he didn't go back to his cabin. Instead, he went to Stan's house and pounded on the door until a petite woman with thin, blonde hair and a wide nose answered the door with a toddler on her hip.

"Where's Stan?" Riko asked her without preamble.

"Riko," she greeted him.

He didn't remember her, but he never did pay much attention to the girls in school. Except for one. But her scent was undeniably shifter. "Where is Stan?" he repeated.

"He's not here," she told him.

Riko lifted one eyebrow. "And where would he be?"

"I don't know. He was out with some guys from the pack last night and didn't come home. I assume they went hunting for the night."

They were hunting all right. But it wasn't for the usual small game.

"Thanks," he told her, and jogged back down the steps and to his truck.

Throwing his truck into 4-wheel drive to get through the snow, Riko headed to the mountains where he knew he'd find the pack. He'd had a lot of time to think while he was watching over Addi all night, and he'd come to the conclusion that he only had two choices here:

One, he could go to his father's funeral tomorrow, say his goodbyes and hightail it back to Oklahoma where he belonged. Then hope like hell she was right, and the pack wouldn't go after her after he was gone.

Or two, he stayed right here in this shit for nothing town, even if she never spoke to him again. But at least he could watch over her that way. At least he would know she was alive. And the way he figured it, he owed her one.

Out of those two, Riko knew there was only one way he could ensure nothing would happen to her. It wasn't his first choice, but it would have to do since she wanted nothing to do with him now, and he couldn't see any way he'd be able to convince her to take him up on his offer to come with him.

Pulling out his cell phone, Riko opened the screen, and then realized he'd never gotten her number. With a curse, he threw his phone on the seat beside him. He had no idea what he would've said. She probably wouldn't even answer the phone. But he just needed the reassurance of hearing her voice, just once, before doing what he was about to do.

This time when he got to the trails, he pulled his truck as close to the woods as he could. Walking around to the passenger side, he left his clothes in the cab and shifted. The trick would be shifting back later in the day when there might be more people coming out to enjoy the new snow.

If he made it back.

He caught the scent of Stan and the other wolves about a half mile off the trail and followed it back to the cave where they'd taken him the day before. Had it only been a day? So much had happened since then, it seemed longer.

When he reached the outskirts of their camp, he walked right in. There was no reason to be sneaky about it. The wind was at his back. They'd probably scented him coming way before he got there. Stan and the three wolves who'd gone after Addison stood at the mouth of the cave, ears alert.

Stan, the largest wolf and the one with the most attitude, stepped forward and bared his teeth as Riko entered the clearing. He knew why Riko was there. The dominant way he'd walked onto their territory in his wolf form had told them all they needed to know. He was there to fight for the coveted position of alpha. And if it was a fair fight, they all knew he'd get it.

The thing was, Stan wasn't dominant enough to handle even this size of a pack for any period of time. The rest of the wolves were playing nice right now and going along with him because the previous alpha wasn't even in the ground yet. But once he was, there was going to be a long, hard road for the pack to find another alpha. The only wolf who had what it took was Riko, and they all knew it. One problem: wolves didn't take kindly to someone leaving the pack like he had all those years before. And if that wolf wanted to come back into the pack? Well, it was possible, sure. If he could survive the re-initiation.

Riko returned Stan's snarl, keeping half an eye on the three wolves behind him. He wouldn't put it past them to gang up on him and then lie about the outcome of the fight just to keep him out of the pack. These four had always had some weird kind of bromance going on back when they were all in high school. Pete, Andy, and Paul had been Stan's bitches back then, and it appeared nothing had changed. And with the rest of the pack at home riding out the snowstorm in front of their fires, they'd get away with it.

However, there was no way in hell Riko was going to lose this fight—fairly or not—and leave Addison here alone to try to protect herself. And he couldn't risk waiting until the entire pack was together to make it happen. But just in case there was anyone else around, he threw his head back and let out a long howl. If anyone else was in the vicinity, they'd come running. Maybe he was too jaded from being gone for so long, but he knew how this pack worked back in the day, and he had a hard time believing they'd let something like knowing Addison her entire life get in the way of doing what they felt they had to do to protect themselves.

As Riko's howl echoed through the trees, Stan froze, the three behind him exchanging nervous glances. But he recovered quickly. In a flash, he was running up on Riko and going for his throat.

Riko blocked him by going up on his hind legs and took Stan to the ground, but he wiggled away before he could get a good grip on him and got back up on his feet. The other three spread out around them in a large circle and barked encouragement to their friend as he walked around Riko, feeling him out.

But Riko didn't believe in giving him time to recoup and was on Stan again as soon as he had his paws under him. They went down to the snow in a ball of teeth and fur, one of them on top and then the other as the two wolves both tried to get the upper hand.

Something big and heavy rammed Riko from behind, teeth clacking in his ear as it went for the meat between his neck and shoulder. Riko dropped to the snow and rolled out of the way as the wolf fell forward, losing its grip. Jumping to his feet, he whirled around, snapping at the wolf. Blood tinged the snow red. His blood. As the scent filled the air around them, the other two came in for a quick kill, and Riko went down.

He gave as good as got, though. His only focus staying alive to protect Addi. If he could just get one wolf off of him, the largest one, he could take the other three.

Ignoring the bites of the smaller wolves, Riko rose to his feet and went after Stan. Blood dripped in his eyes and stained his fur, but he didn't stop until Stan was on the ground on his back and Riko's teeth were around his throat. Right at that moment, four other wolves ran up onto the scene. Two of them jumped into the fight and ripped the smaller wolves off of Riko's back. Growling and baring their teeth, they forced them back when they tried to go around to save their friend.

This was the way it should be. Riko had every right to make this a fight to the death for the way they'd all acted, but more dead wolves meant taking these idiots away from their families, and Riko didn't want to do that.

Tightening his hold, he waited until Stan whimpered his surrender before releasing him. Backing off, he let him get up, the coppery taste of blood on his tongue hard to resist, but didn't take his eye off of him until he was sure Stan wasn't going to pull any more shit.

Lowering his head nearly to the ground, Stan crept up to his new alpha and gave him his throat. Riko bit him without pressure and let him go so he could slink off to get condolences from his buddies. The four new wolves who'd arrived late on the scene came up to him and did the same, and then the three who had ganged up on him, noticeably more timid than the rest.

Riko was glad protocol didn't have him going to them. He stood with his legs locked straight and his back ramrod stiff so he didn't fall over. Once they'd all accepted his dominance, Riko inhaled deep and howled to the sky, announcing to all who could hear who their new alpha was. He didn't worry that the entire pack wasn't there. Word would travel fast, and if anyone else wanted to challenge him they could do it at the next pack meeting.

Shortly after, the others took off into the woods and Riko hobbled his way back to his truck, lying low within the trees until he was sure no humans were around to see him shift back. It took him three tries to get his pants on and he couldn't tie his boots, but eventually he was dressed and back on the road.

His first thought was to get to Addison and make sure Stan hadn't pulled some crap while he kept Riko busy, but one look in the rearview mirror told him he should go home and clean up first. However, he couldn't shake the feeling that something was wrong. Maybe it was just his own paranoia, but he'd never forgive himself if she was hurt, or worse, while he was getting pretty in the shower.

By the time he pulled into town, Riko was revved up and ready for another fight, his hands shaking on the steering wheel and his foot heavy on the gas. He went right to Addi's house and pulled into her driveway. Leaving the engine running, he threw himself out of the truck, falling to one knee in the snow before getting up and rushing onto the porch and yanking open the screen door.

"Addi!" he roared as he pounded on the storm door. He tried the knob, but it was locked. "Addison! Open the fucking door!"

He was about to knock again when the door opened and Addison's father stood there. His faded hazel eyes took one look at Riko and he called over his shoulder, "Addison! It's for you!"

"I'm not home!" she yelled from the back of the house.

"Oh, I think you should be for this," her father yelled back, grinning at Riko. Quieter, he asked, "You okay, son?"

Riko blinked, still a bit stunned it hadn't been Addi who'd opened the door. Then realizing he was waiting for an answer, he gave him a nod. "Yes, sir. I think so."

Addison's father nodded back. "Stay on the porch. I don't want blood all over the floor in here."

"Yeah, okay."

"And good luck," he whispered right as Addison appeared beside him. With a wink, he walked away, whistling loudly.

Riko backed up and gave Addi room to come outside with him, his head swimming with relief that she was safe and alive. She stared at him a moment, then she grabbed her coat from the hook and came outside, closing the door behind her. "What happened to you?" she asked.

"It doesn't matter. I just wanted to check on you, and let you know that you're safe now."

She stared at him. "What does that mean?"

"It means I'm leaving tomorrow right after the funeral, but I wanted you to know that you don't have to worry. I took care of everything." He thought about explaining what happened, and what he had to do now, but in the end, he just said, "Take care of yourself, Addison." Then he limped across the porch and down the steps to the yard. If he stayed there any longer, he'd just end up making an ass of himself. She'd made it quite clear what she thought about him and his kind. And after today, she wouldn't ever have to see him anymore.

"Riko, wait!"

Addison stopped him before he got back into his truck. He turned back, his body humming with adrenaline and the need to get the fuck out of there.

One hand on the door handle, Riko glared at her. He didn't like her seeing this side of him. Call it pride or ego or some other idiotic male shit, but he didn't want her to see him as weak.

Heart pounding a rapid staccato, he watched as she fought her way through the snow. It had started coming down harder again since he'd been there.

When she reached him, Riko waited for her to say something. To tell him to stay. Give him something, anything, to give him hope that all wasn't completely lost between them. But as he stood there staring down at her, watching her expressions change as her eyes traveled over his bloodied face, he knew that he would never hold her in his arms again.

"Have a safe trip," she finally said. And then she turned and walked away, and his heart became as frozen as the snow, cracking in a way he knew he'd never be able to fix.

CHAPTER 10

Back inside her house, Addison watched Riko leave. She was worried about him. There was what looked like a bite wound on his jaw and claw marks on his forehead that disappeared into his hairline. Streaks of blood covered his face, neck, and hands. He looked like he'd bled a lot. And what about infection?

Yet those same wounds also slammed it home to her exactly what he was.

A heavy hand settled on her shoulder, and she looked over to see her father standing beside her. "Don't worry too much about him," he told her. "He'll be all right in a few hours."

Addison frowned. "What do you mean?"

"He'll heal right up," he said with a smile, then he leaned down closer to her ear and lowered his voice. "Those wolves are some pretty sturdy people." Then he turned his face away from the window and winked at her. Patting her shoulder, she watched as he wandered over to the stove to make his oatmeal, the same thing he'd had for breakfast for as long as she could remember.

"Dad, how do you know about that?"

"About what?" he said over his shoulder. Then he smiled.

Not knowing what else to say, Addison sank into one of the kitchen chairs. Her father knew about these things? When? How?

A few minutes later, he brought his bowl over and joined her. "Don't look so surprised, honey. A man doesn't live to be my age in this small of a town without finding out a few secrets about the locals."

She was suddenly angry. "And you never thought of sharing this with me?"

"Oh, don't you go puffing all up on me, now. It was safer for you not to know."

Crossing her arms over her chest, she sank back against the chair. She was acting like she was seventeen again, but she couldn't help it. "Did you know about Riko?" she asked him after a long silence.

Her father nodded as he took a spoonful of oatmeal, then wiped his mouth with his napkin. "Sure, sure I did. I also knew about what you two were doing back then."

Addison felt her face heat, and not from anger this time. "Dad—"

But he waved away what she was about to say. "Ah, honey. Don't think nothing of it. Riko's a good boy, in spite of how his father raised him. A little bit of a rascal sometimes—"

She harrumphed. "All the time."

"All the time," he corrected. "But he was a good boy. And he's grown into a good man."

"He's not a man," she said quietly.

Wielding his spoon at her, he gave her his "stern" face. "Yes, he is. He just so happens to be a man who happens to be a bit...more than we are. It's not his fault. He was born that way. And you shouldn't discriminate against him because of it."

Shocked that her own father would say something like that to her, her mouth gaped open. "I'm not discriminating against him!"

"Then what do you call what you've been doing since you found out about him?"

Addison had a comeback all ready, but then she snapped her mouth shut and sighed. "That's not why," she told him. "Not totally why. I'm just using it as an excuse to get him to leave."

"Do you really want him to leave?"

"Yes." No.

He grabbed a toothpick out of the jar at the center of the table, leaned back in his chair, and lifted one scraggly eyebrow at her.

"He asked me to go with him," she confessed. "Right before all of...this." She waved her hand in the air to indicate Riko showing up on their porch that morning, twice, everything that had happened since he'd come back home, and the people who lived in the small town overall and everything that came with them.

"And you turned him down."

She looked at him in surprise. "Of course I turned him down."

Her father chewed on his toothpick for a minute while he stared down at his empty bowl. "Why?" he finally asked her.

"Why?" She couldn't quite keep the disbelief out of her voice.

"That's what I asked."

Addison frowned. "I can't just up and leave."

"Why not?"

"Because I have a job. I have you..."

He shook his head. "Ah, honey. Don't you go giving up on happiness because of me. I'm an old man, but I'm not on death's door. I'll still be here for a bit. It's not like you couldn't visit."

She reached over and took his hand, squeezing it in her own. "I know that."

"Then what's stopping you?"

But she couldn't tell him. There were so many things, and what had happened last night and this morning were just the tip of the iceberg. "He's just not the guy for me, Dad."

Pulling his hand from hers, her father cupped her face in his hand like he used to do when she was little. "I wouldn't be so sure about that. But it's your decision. You're a big girl. You can make up your own mind." With a smile, he got up to wash out his bowl and put it into the drainer for tomorrow.

Addison looked out the window, but the snow had stopped.

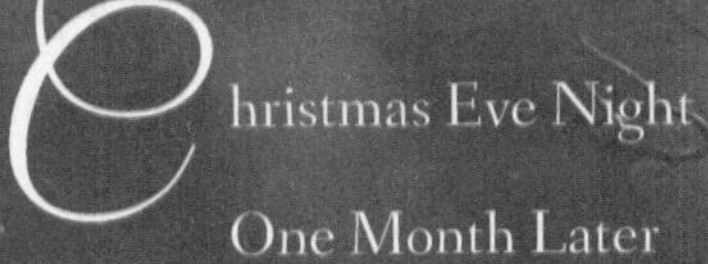

CHAPTER 11

Christmas Eve Night

One Month Later

Riko pulled his truck over to the side of the road just down the street from Addi's house, the gift he'd brought her on the seat beside him. Turning off the engine, he sat for a minute, going over and over in his head what he was going to say.

If she'd even give him enough time to say anything at all before she slammed the door in his face.

He hadn't meant to be gone so long, but it had taken him more time than he'd thought it would to wrap up things with his alpha in Oklahoma and then get back here and get this pack under control. He'd brought a couple of guys back with him—wolves he could trust—so he'd needed to get them settled, too.

Also, he'd decided not to stay in town this time, and he'd done that on purpose so as not to run into Addi. He didn't want to cause her any more stress, so he'd spent most of his time at the hotel outside of town or in the mountains with his new pack. But being so close to her and not being able to be *with* her was taking its toll. He was distracted, and that was dangerous, both for him as the new alpha and for his pack.

He'd still been willing to ride it out, though. After all, he'd lived without her for twenty years before he'd come back here. Seeing her again, however, had hit him harder than an avalanche. And after a long chat with his old alpha, Riko decided he'd been a fool to leave her here the first time, and an even bigger ass to walk out on her again, though at least the second time couldn't really be avoided. There were things he'd had to take care of before he could turn his focus to her. Plus, she'd more or less told him to go. But come hell or high water, he wasn't going to let her push him away again.

Addi was made for him, human or not, and he couldn't walk away without making one last plea that she give the two of them a real chance. Hopefully, now that she'd had some time to come to grips with his big reveal— unintended as it had been—she wouldn't be so repulsed by him.

Taking a deep breath, he got out of the truck and closed the door, remembered he'd left her gift on the seat, and jogged around to the passenger side to get it. He'd just closed the door and locked the truck when his shifter hearing picked up the creak of a door.

His eyes flew to Addison's house just in time to see her walk out onto the porch. She was wearing some kind of loose pants with candy canes all over them, snow boots, and had a long, bulky gray sweater wrapped tight against the cold. Her long, dark hair was loose on her shoulders. Piano notes drifted out the screen door from inside the house. Swaying back and forth to the music, she danced her way to the edge of the porch, the movements slow and sad.

As he watched, Addison held out one hand, catching a few snowflakes on her palm as it started to snow. She smiled a little, but it wasn't a real smile. It was a smile without happiness or hope, only resignation. She wiped at one cheek and began to sway back and forth to the song again, her beautiful eyes staring at something he couldn't see. White Christmas lights flickered on around her as the sun set, strung along the rooftop and porch railing.

She was a vision, like something out of a fairytale, and Riko couldn't stop staring at her.

As the snow began to fall harder, she lifted her eyes to the sky to watch it come down. Then she stopped dancing and held perfectly still, all except for her head, which turned slowly in his direction.

Riko lifted his free hand and waved, then started across the road, hoping against hope she wouldn't run back inside and leave him standing out there in the cold. Addi watched him come, her posture stiff. "Hey," he said when he was standing below her.

Her eyes travelled over his face for a long moment before they dropped to the gift he held. "Who is that?"

Riko glanced down at the calf in his arm. She looked back up at him with soft brown eyes that looked too big in her soft, buttermilk face. Her long legs hung nearly to his knees, and her hide was soft as silk. "She's for you. I thought she could keep Mistletoe company."

Addi wrapped her arms around her stomach. "What am I supposed to name her?"

"Whatever you want," he told her softly.

She looked down at the calf, who was trying to lick Riko's face with her long, warm tongue. "How about Gingerbread? We could call her Ginger for short."

We. She'd said *we.* "I like that. It suits her."

"Where did you get her?"

"I brought her back with me from Oklahoma. Her momma—" Riko cut himself off. Addison didn't need to know what had happened.

The beginnings of a frown started wrinkling her forehead, and Riko threw up his free hand to stop what he knew she had to be thinking. "I didn't eat her!" he swore. "I didn't. She survived the virus with a few others on a farm a friend of mine found out about. She had this baby, and then got killed in an accident. An honest to God accident, involving large farm equipment and details I really don't want to go into."

Addison looked as though she didn't know whether or not to believe him. "Well, you might as well put her down. She'll figure her way out through the fence soon enough anyway. I'll let everyone know they can't eat her, either."

"Or I can just fix your barn and threaten anyone who comes near her."

A ghost of a smile played around Addi's mouth. "Or that."

Riko smiled as he set Ginger down so she could explore the yard. "She's still bottle-fed. I've got everything in the truck. I know you have to work and that, but I can help if you need it. Just let me know."

A look of confusion passed over her beautiful face. "How are you going to do that? You don't live here."

"I do now," he told her. Then he watched her carefully for her reaction.

She stilled. "What?"

Riko glanced over to check on Ginger, who was bowling over some deer decorations as she chased snowflakes, before he responded. "That day...that last day you saw me..." He wondered how much he should tell her, but in the end, he decided to be brief and he could fill her in on the details later if she cared to know them. "I became alpha of the wolf pack that day. So, this is my home now. Again." He shrugged.

Addi didn't say anything for a long time, and when she did, it wasn't at all what he'd expected. "So, you're not here to ask me to run away with you? Again," she mimicked.

Riko's heart began to pound. "Would you? If I asked?"

She looked down at the porch and bit her lip. When she raised her eyes, there were tears in them. "I don't know, to be honest."

That was all Riko needed to join her on the porch, making it to her in three long strides. Clenching his fists at his sides to keep from reaching for her, he had to clear his throat before he could speak. "Addi, it's never been anyone but you for me. Do you know that?"

He could see the doubt on her face.

"I swear it. I tried to forget you. I really did. And honestly, I thought I had, but—"

She looked away, and he gently pulled her face back around and waited until she looked up at him. "But the moment I saw you again, it was like the last twenty years just slipped away. You're my everything, Addison Conley. Even when you weren't with me, you were in my dreams. I'd smell your hair in the wind and feel your touch on my skin. I'd hear your voice in the trees when the seasons changed. But when I'd look, you weren't there." His voice broke, and he swallowed hard. "I left you because I wanted to protect you. Not because I wanted to. Please, believe me."

"And now?" she asked after a long moment.

Riko rubbed his thumb over the smooth skin of her cheek and then took her hand. "Now, I'm asking you to give me a second chance." He didn't go into the fact that he howled at the moon whenever the mood struck him, or all of the pack politics that he was working on changing. None of that mattered. At least not to him. And if Addison would just...*be* with him, they could work everything else out.

Addi looked down at their hands. Riko waited. And waited. But she didn't say anything.

Well, guess that was his answer then, wasn't it? He brought her hand to his mouth and kissed the inside of her palm, then cleared his throat and released her. "Okay. I get it." Rubbing his eyes with the heel of his hand, he backed off. "I'll just get out of your way. If you need help with Ginger, I can send somebody over."

"What are you doing?"

He looked up to find her staring at him in confusion.

"Uh...leaving?"

"No, Riko. You're not."

He picked up on a thread of fear in her voice, and a flash of hope shot through him. "I'm not?"

She shook her head. "No."

The smile that broke out across his face hurt his cheeks it was so big. "I'm not leaving."

"No," she repeated. Closing the distance between them, she reached out to touch him, but then dropped her hand as she said, "I'm sorry I've been such a bitch."

Riko wished she would try to touch him again. "Aw, that just makes you the perfect mate for a wolf."

It took her a minute to get the joke, but when she did, her laugh was the most beautiful thing Riko had ever heard, and he vowed to make her do that more often.

As her laughter faded, she glanced up at him. "So, are you gonna kiss me or what?"

"Yes, ma'am," he told her gruffly.

Her hands crept beneath his shirt to touch the bare skin of his abs as he pulled her in closer. Riko shuddered as they slid softly over his stomach and around to his sides where she gripped him tight. Cupping her jaw in his hand, he lifted her face and captured her mouth with his.

He'd wanted to take it slow, savor things, but the moment he felt her mouth soft and pliant beneath his, he growled deep in his throat and kissed her with all of the urgency and fear and pain that had been riding him since the day she'd told him to leave.

Addi moaned in response and pressed closer, her soft curves fitting against him perfectly and her arms wrapping around his waist.

Riko kissed and nipped his way down her throat to the sensitive spot between her neck and shoulder, one hand gripped in her hair and other low on her back, pulling her hips tight against him. She felt so good in his arms. So sweet. So soft. And somewhere within the haze of love and lust he was drowning in, Riko realized something...

He was home.

Thank you so much for reading Riko and Addie's story, the kickoff to my new Snow Ridge Shifters series! I hope you enjoyed it. More books in the series will be coming your way in 2022. But if you want more shifters now, check out The Kincaid Werewolves, my sexy Scottish werewolves who have a soft spot for curvy Fae women.
The series is complete, starting with:
Lone Wolf's Claim
And if you want to sign up for my newsletter to be the

first to hear about new releases, giveaways, free books, and other odds and ends, you can do so here:
Sign Up for L.E.'s newsletter
I have to be honest, I try to email twice a month, but they can be a little sporadic sometimes. However, I promise to keep them full of awesome stuff.
Thank you again for reading!

L.E. Wilson writes romance starring intense alpha males and the women who are fearless enough to tame them — for the most part anyway. ;) In her novels you'll find smoking hot scenes, a touch of suspense, some humor, a bit of gore, and multifaceted characters, all working together to combine her lifelong obsession with the paranormal and her love of romance.

Her writing career came about the usual way: on a dare from her loving husband. Little did she know just one casual suggestion would open a box of worms (or words as the case may be) that would forever change her life.

Lattes and music are a necessary part of her writing process, though sometimes you'll find her typing away at her favorite Starbucks. She walks two miles to get there, to make up for all of those coffees.

On a Personal Note:

"I love to hear from my readers! Contact me anytime at le@lewilsonauthor.com."

Keep In Touch With L.E.
lewilsonauthor.com
le@lewilsonauthor.com

facebook.com/LEWilsonAuthor

instagram.com/LEWilsonAuthor

bookbub.com/authors/l-e-wilson

tiktok.com/@LEWilsonAuthor